Fred & Anthony

Meet

THE DEMENTED SUPER-DEGERM-O ZOMBIE

By ESILE AREVAMIRP

With ELISE PRIMAVERA

Hyperion Books for Children/New York

This book is dedicated to my brother Tom,
who definitely has OCSDD tendencies.

Text and illustrations copyright © 2007 by Elise Primavera

First Edition
1 3 5 7 9 10 8 6 4 2

Printed in the United States of America
ISBN-13: 978-0-7868-3679-6
ISBN-10: 0-7868-3679-2
Library of Congress Cataloging-in-Publication Data on file.
Reinforced binding
Visit www.hyperionbooksforchildren.com

RAINDROPS KEEP FALLING ON MY HEAD Words by Hal David; Music by Burt Bacharach
@ 1969 (Renewed 1997) NEW HIDDEN VALLEY MUSIC, CASA DAVID and WB MUSIC CORP.
All rights reserved. Used by permission of ALFRED PUBLISHING CO., INC.
RAINDROPS KEEP FALLING ON MY HEAD From BUTCH CASSIDY AND THE SUNDANCE KID
Lyrics by Hal David; Music by Burt Bacharach @ 1969 (Renewed) Casa David, New Hidden
Valley Music, and WB Music Corp. International Copyright Secured. All rights reserved.

DISCLAIMER:
This book contains references to a condition called OCSDD (Obsessive-Compulsive
Super-Degerm-O Disorder). In no way are we making light of this illness. However, if you feel the
need to write an angry letter to us you probably have every right, although we would recommend
counseling if you feel the need to shower more than once and write a lot of angry letters.

CONTENTS

This book is the second in a series of however many it takes for these boys to make enough serious dough so that they will forever be able to pay someone else to do their work for them while they watch horror movies and eat Pez and Chex Mix. It is highly recommended that you and everyone in our solar system buy and read the first Fred and Anthony book. For the few cheapskates—I mean kids—who have not, here is a short summary of *FRED & ANTHONY'S ESCAPE FROM THE NETHERWORLD*.

THE HORRIBLE HIDEOUS MONDAY MORNING

The boys managed to avoid most, if not every, kind of work by paying someone else to do it for them.

YES, IT'S THE OCSDD* GHOST, LADIES AND GENTLEMEN—LOCK YOUR DOORS AND HIDE YOUR HOOVERS!

But for the first time in their young lives one horrible, hideous Monday morning, they realized that the horrible, hideous history project from the first book had never gotten done, and it was due that very day!

*If you don't know what this is, you skipped the fine print on page 2. Go back and read it, we'll wait here for you.

With light backpacks and heavy hearts, the boys made their way to school.

Fred and Anthony were about to come face-to-face with the horrible, hideous history teacher.

He was so vile, so mean . . . and yet there was the slightest tinge of a lemony-fresh scent about him.

Still, mere mortals quaked at the very mention of his name.

Mr. Bomzie, the fourth-grade history teacher, had a strange preoccupation with personal hygiene and was the only man equipped with a brain capable of concocting hideous history project after hideous history project. Was he even *human*?

As Fred and Anthony entered the classroom, they couldn't shake the feeling that they were in very much the same predicament as the rebellious, unstable young man in the movie *It's Alive 119: It Died Yet Lived* when he went out to investigate strange noises, even though he knew a pumpkin-headed slasher was on the loose.

DO YOU THINK IT'S POSSIBLE FOR A FOURTH GRADER TO DIE OF A HEART ATTACK?

OH, COME ON. WHAT'S THE WORST THING THAT COULD HAPPEN?

FRED ¿
ANTHONY
FAIL
HISTORY

And that's not all. They were never ever, ever, EVER allowed to ever see another horror movie ever again; Fred was never ever, ever, EVER allowed to eat Pez; and his glowing-skull dispenser and Anthony's stash of Chex Mix were thrown into a steamer trunk, which was hermetically sealed and hidden in some undisclosed location.

When they weren't at school, they were locked inside Fred's basement, where they were forced to finally make the Alamo out of Popsicle sticks, in addition to Mount Rushmore out of sugar cubes, and Washington crossing the Delaware out of elbow macaroni.

Fred and Anthony dropped their sugar cubes, and with the superhuman strength that comes only when you hear a bloodcurdling scream, they managed to break open the basement door.

SO, YOU ALWAYS CARRY A BOBBY PIN?

YEAH, DON'T YOU?

HELP! HELP!

The boys raced to the kitchen, where the voice was coming from, and sure enough, there was Fred's grandmother, clutching her DustBuster, cowering in the corner with fright. Which actually wasn't all that surprising, because over by the sink, washing her hands, was a ghost—in fact, it was Fred and Anthony's ghost.

27

A QUICK QUIZ

1. The OCSDD Ghost was in my bedroom the other night and . . .

   a.) the bed levitated four feet off the ground and spun in a counterclockwise circle.

   b.) the walls pulsated, and green slime formed on the ceiling.

   c.) my carpet was steam-cleaned, and all my shirts were pressed.

2. The OCSDD Ghost was wearing . . .

   a.) a bedsheet.

   b.) a Tommy Bahamas Shirt.

   c.) a biohazard suit.

KEEP GOING

3. While the OCSDD Ghost was here I experienced . . .

a.) uncontrollable projectile vomiting.

b.) oozing sores, and my brains fell out of my head.

c.) a strange compulsion to wash my hands over and over and over and over and over and over and over.

4. After the OCSDD Ghost left . . .

a.) I collapsed on the floor and dialed 911.

b.) I went to the nearest Motel 6, where I've been ever since.

c.) He hasn't—every time he tries to leave, he comes back to check to see if he left the oven on.

Meanwhile . . . just as Fred knew that the feisty flamenco-dancing short-order cook would escape his possessed kitchen appliances in *Bolivian Blue-Plate Blood Freak*, Fred knew that his and Anthony's crummy lives were about to take a turn for the better.

DON'T WORRY, GRANDMA! I WILL USE EVERY FIBER OF MY BEING TO GET TO THE BOTTOM OF THIS!

HE SAID "BOTTOM."

While the boys were chasing their own ghost out of the kitchen, the *real* OCSDD ghost had struck again! But he was no match for Fred and Anthony.

Yes, the boys would soon be leaving the corner of Doggie-doo Avenue and Barfbreath Lane behind.

Why? Fred suddenly had a fantastic idea.

Fred told Anthony how it was just like in the movie *Schizoid Zombies Who Came to Life and Became Mixed-Up Prisoners of Alcatraz*, where the falsely accused prisoner makes friends with the schizoid zombie and the falsely accused prisoner gets the schizoid zombie to scare the evil warden so that he, the falsely accused prisoner, is the only one in all of Alcatraz who can save the evil warden, so the evil warden sets the falsely accused prisoner free. . . .

SO WE JUST APPLY THAT TO OUR SITUATION—GET IT?

NO.

Fred and Anthony could haunt *every* house in town—and then charge the owners to get rid of the ghost.

At long last, their wildest dreams were about to come true.

I'M GOING TO HAVE THE FINEST ITALIAN CRAFTSMEN BUILD A GIANT 24-KARAT GOLD-PLATED PEZ DISPENSER THAT WILL DELIVER A NEVER-ENDING EVERY-FLAVORED SUPPLY OF PEZ ON AND ON INTO INFINITY.

I WILL NO LONGER HAVE TO WORK IN OBSCURITY WRITING THESE STUPID CHAPTER BOOKS. I CAN WRITE MY OWN BOOKS, AND, FOR THE FIRST TIME IN MY AFTERLIFE, BECOME POPULAR!

43

Fred and Anthony and their ghost were ready for Mr. Bomzie. It was only a matter of time, they figured, before their horrible, hideous history teacher would be screaming for his mommy.

As it turned out, Fred and Anthony were half right. Mr. Bomzie *was* screaming—but it

was not "Mommy"—it was "Colonial Williamsburg
. . . made out of paper plates and Q-tips . . . due
next Friday . . . or else."

The worst had happened. If the boys were
ever going to get out of the basement to see
the light of day, immediately followed by
returning to the basement to see a really
gross horror movie, they were going to have to
straighten up and fly right, roll up their
sleeves, pull up their socks, and get to work.

Fred and Anthony's happy days of goofing
off and watching horror movies were over.

IT'S TOO HORRIBLE.

DON'T LISTEN TO THAT
GARBAGE. IT'S NOT
OVER UNTIL THE FAT
LADY SINGS.

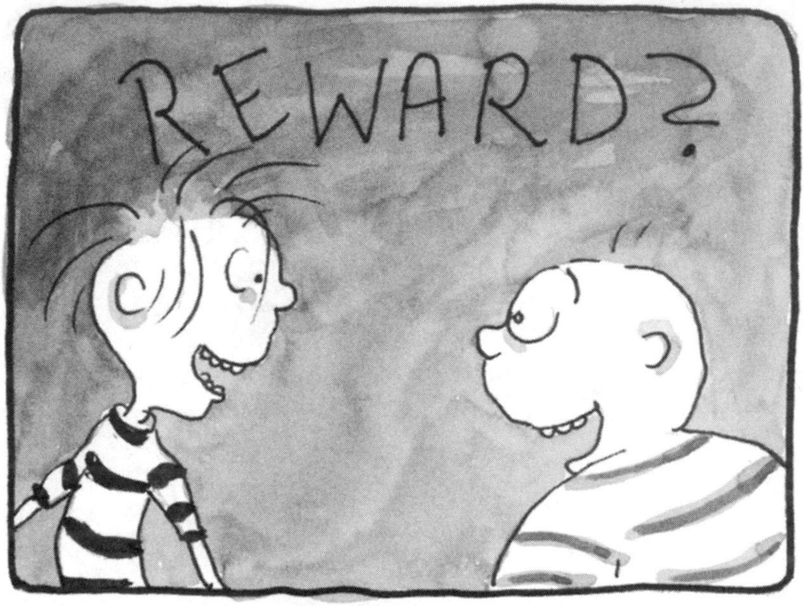
REWARD?

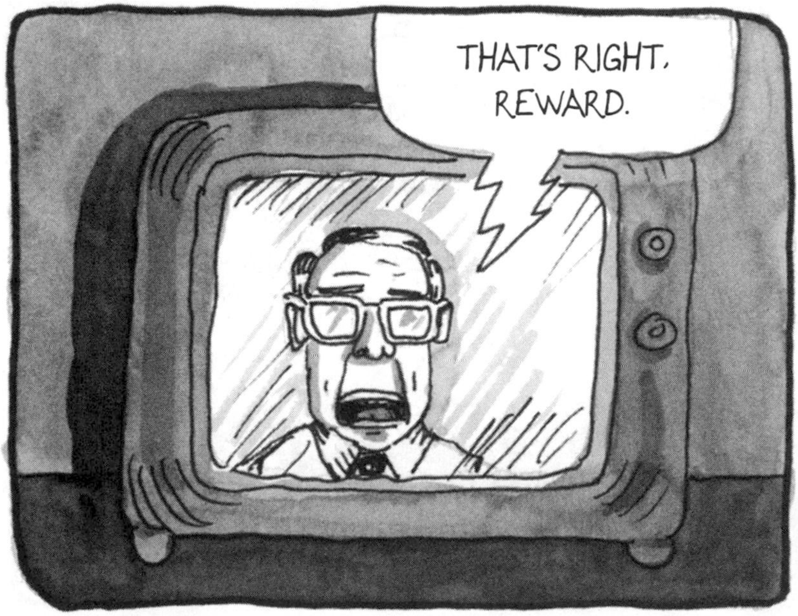
THAT'S RIGHT, REWARD.

Fred and Anthony's hopes and dreams, as well as their chances of reaching fifth grade before middle age, had spiraled down that great big toilet bowl of life. But one thing that could never be flushed away was their good old Fred and Anthony spirit!

Without a shadow of a doubt, Fred and Anthony knew that they and only they were capable of catching the OCSDD Ghost.

The boys left immediately, feeling as though a power greater than themselves was directing them. In keeping with this theme, the condos were easy to find, too—all they had to do was follow the trail of those little white things. But upon reaching their final destination, Fred and Anthony's optimism soon faded.

WELCOME to THE OTHER SIDE OF THE TRACKS!

51

GUIDE TO THE NETHERWORLD

Points of Interest:

If you've already visited the Netherworld, here are some other places to see!

Candy & Flowers Condos— otherwise known as Maniac Towers— has a lemony fresh scent, but don't be deceived. If you happen to come across this point of interest, we advise you to turn around and run as fast as you can away from it.

THESE AREN'T LITTLE WHITE THINGS!

THEY'RE COTTON BALLS!

That's right, kids—cotton balls. And they weren't just *ordinary* cotton balls either—they were Fred's *grandmother's* cotton balls! Which could only mean one thing—and if you have been able to follow this story so far, you would know what that is!

Against their ghost's, and probably any reasonably sane person's, better judgment, Fred and Anthony raced into the unusually antiseptic-looking apartment building. They headed straight for the elevator and stepped inside.

59

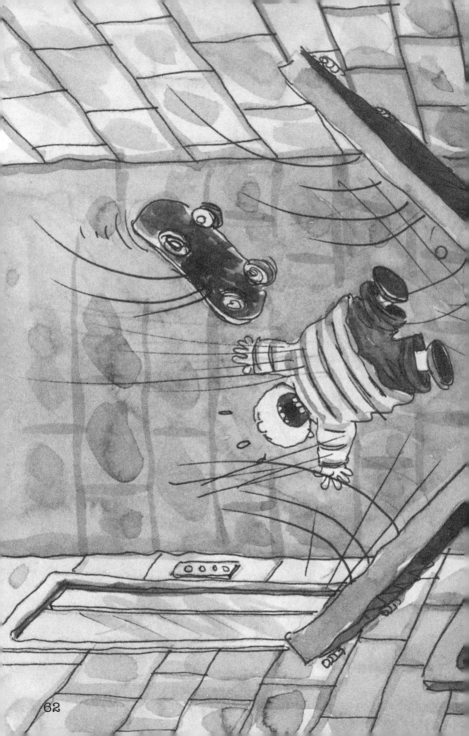

65

THE GIANT SLIMY SNOT-SANDWICH–EATING FUNGUS BLOB

Fred and Anthony recognized him immediately because they had seen the movie: *The Giant Slimy Snot-Sandwich–Eating Fungus Blob! The Musical!*

Fred and Anthony had ended up inside what appeared to be a very clean condo. There wasn't a speck of dirt, dust, or blood and guts anywhere—which was a problem for the Giant Slimy Snot-Sandwich–Eating Fungus Blob, who lived there.

Usually docile, he was the angriest, most upset Fungus Blob Fred and Anthony had ever seen. In fact, he was so angry he felt like killing something. Two somethings, actually— Fred and Anthony, in fact.

I KEEP COMING HOME TO A SPOTLESSLY CLEAN CONDO, AND IT'S DRIVING ME NUTS—YOU CAN SEE FOR YOURSELVES—THERE'S NOT A DROP OF BLOOD AND GUTS OR SNOT OR ANYTHING!
THE OCSDD GHOST STRIKES AGAIN.

In their tireless pursuit of the OCSDD Ghost, Fred and Anthony wasted no time and crept inside what appeared to be another very clean condo. There wasn't a drop of blood and guts or snot anywhere here, either!

There *was*, however, a pile of elbow macaroni, a pile of sugar cubes, a pile of paper towel tubes, and a lot of other stuff—plus the cotton balls and the hermetically sealed trunk with Fred's Pez and Anthony's Chex Mix locked inside.

From behind a pile of kitchen sinks, dressed from head to toe in a biohazard suit and counting Fred's grandmother's cotton balls, was . . .

77

OR PERHAPS YOU'D LIKE TO WHITTLE A QUICK MODEL OF BETSY ROSS'S HOUSE OUT OF AN IVORY SOAP BAR?
SOAP

I'M MR. BOMZIE, THE DS ZOMBIE!

OBSESSIVE COMPULSIVE DEMENTED SUPER—DEGERM-O DSD For Short

THE OCDSD ZOMBIE

"HA! HA! HA! HA! HA!" the DSD Zombie laughed maniacally. "Boys! They never wash their hands—or anything else for that matter! They're nothing more than wiggly germ factories on legs . . . sticky-fingered microbe machines spewing out nasty bacteria, viruses, and disease.

"I must sanitize every boy on the face of the earth with my Super Duper O-Boyo-Degerm-O Solution—otherwise known as boiling hot hydrogen peroxide!"

"But then there won't be any boys left—just girls!" Fred cried.

"I'll get *them* too!" The DSD Zombie snickered malevolently.

The DSD Zombie lunged for the boys and it looked like they were goners, but there was a bigger problem. Because while it was true that Fred and Anthony were being held captive by a twisted, cleanliness-obsessed zombie who was about to super-sanitize them to death in his O-Boyo-Degerm-O Solution, there was still something else that was very, very wrong. . . .

If you will remember, the boys were writing this series of chapter books in order to make them richer than the queen of England. But let's face it, the only thing really worth reading about is ghosts, monsters, and blood and guts, not cotton balls and Degerm-O Solution.

83

85

THE STUPID CHAPTER BOOK WITCH

Luckily, the Stupid Chapter Book Witch—who had oodles of knowledge, not to mention an extraordinary, bordering-on-insane love of children's literature—arrived in the nick of time to rescue the plot of Fred and Anthony's story.

WHEN I GET MY HANDS ON THEM, I'M GOING TO PUT THEM IN A ROOM AND MAKE THEM READ THEIR OWN CHAPTER BOOKS UNTIL THEIR BRAINS TURN TO SLUDGE AND DRIBBLE OUT OF THEIR NOSES!

COME ON, ANTHONY. LET'S GET OUT OF HERE.

OKAY, FRED.

ANTHONY?
FRED?

Unluckily, the Stupid Chapter Book Witch was so overwhelmed with emotion by what could possibly be the stupidest chapter book she'd ever seen, she picked up the first thing she could get her hands on, which happened to be the hermetically sealed trunk, and hurled it at the boys.

Luckily, it missed! Fred and Anthony were confident that their lives had been saved. There was only one thing . . .

. . . they couldn't steer. Fred and Anthony plowed right into the Giant Slimy Snot-Sandwich–Eating Fungus Blob, who was coming over to see if they had psychically exterminated his neighbor yet.

It was sort of like plowing into green moldy cat barf and that white stuff in scrambled eggs that you wouldn't eat if your life depended on it.

In anger, the Fungus Blob grabbed the first thing he could get his hands on, which was the Stupid Chapter Book Witch, as well as the DSD Zombie. There were a lot of disgusting gurgling noises and a green lumpy trail of jellied drool, mixed with a stomach-churning lemony-fresh scent.

And then . . .

GLURG!

ARGLE!

The Stupid Chapter Book Witch, as well as the DSD Zombie, was gone.

And so were Fred and Anthony.

Fred and Anthony came to rest beside a charming little cottage by a babbling brook.

They had escaped the DSD Zombie, the Stupid Chapter Book Witch, and the Fungus Blob. They had retrieved Fred's grandmother's cotton balls, and they had the steamer trunk with Fred's Pez and Anthony's Chex Mix.

There was only one *other* thing . . .

It was hermetically sealed—REMEMBER?

GUIDE to the NETHERWORLD

TIP # 6

HERMITS IN THE NETHERWORLD

hen visiting the Netherworld, it is always useful to know where the hermits are. Why? For one thing they will offer food and shelter to just about anybody. They can seal and unseal just about anything, and they make great espresso. Hermits can be found in charming cottages by babbling brooks.

105

In a jiffy, the hermit unsealed Fred and Anthony's steamer trunk, and the boys were able to get their Pez and Chex Mix.

They were invited to stay for bean dip and meet the hermit's friend, who would be there any minute. But Fred knew that his grandmother was anxious to see her cotton balls again, so he and Anthony took a rain check, thanked the kindly hermit, and left.

I FEEL REALLY BAD ABOUT LEAVING.

YEAH, AND I JUST LOVE BEAN DIP.

WHAT DID HE SAY HIS FRIEND'S NAME WAS?

FRANK

GUIDE to the NETHERWORLD TIP #7

In the Netherworld, nicknames are common, as are abbreviations. For example: Drac is short for Dracula, the Wolferino is short for the Wolfman, the Mumster is short for the Mummy, and Frank is short for . . .

Oh, if only Fred and Anthony had just done the horrible, hideous history project—they would be home snug in the basement working on another horrible history project. Instead they were hanging on to life by a thread.

Alas! As we watch the very breath being squizzled and squashed out of our two young heroes, the question still begs to be asked: What can we learn from all this?

BUPKIS!

With the tender touch of a mother's love,
she guided Fred and Anthony to the safety of
Maniac Towers, from where the boys would be
able to find their way back to the bosom of

their families. And if you think the word "bosom" is funny, then you are being very childish—unlike Fred and Anthony, who have matured considerably since this story began.

FINISH

Fred and Anthony were grateful to have once again escaped the Netherworld alive.

Or did they?

13
A STRANGE PHENOMENON OCCURS

After their near death experience, the most remarkable thing happened. All that had ever been horrible and hideous in Fred and Anthony's lives before was now great.

Everybody liked the boys. They had all the horror movies and Pez and Chex Mix they wanted.

The horrible, hideous history teacher was replaced by a heavenly honey of a history teacher, who never gave homework. She let everybody eat Pez and Chex Mix; she never gave tests; and she had a nice fresh scent about her that had nothing to do with lemons.

I'LL NEVER HAVE TO SUFFER AT THE HANDS OF THE HORRIBLE, HIDEOUS HISTORY TEACHER.
THEY SAVED MY SANI-FLUSH.
I REALLY NEEDED THIS JOB—SUCH WONDERFUL BOYS.

123

Fred and Anthony stood on the threshold of the gymnasium, just before phys. ed. class, wondering if they were alive or dead. Could it be that they were in some weird, bizarro alternate reality?

Could it be they were just like the cocky astronauts in the movie *Alien 147: They Thought They Were Alive, But They Really Weren't?*

No. At last they were certain. They *were* still alive and thankful beyond words. Things were just as bad as they'd ever been! For what could be more horrible or hideous than . . .